The Inconvenient God

The Inconvenient God

Francesca Forrest

AnnorlundaBooks

Front cover illustration and design by Likhain.

Editing services from Nerine Dorman.

Published in the United States by Annorlunda Books.

Queries: info@annorlundaenterprises.com

First Edition

ISBN-13: 978-1-944354-41-1

"I'm so glad you're here, madam, so glad we're finally taking care of this...problem," said Mr. Haksola, the slight, middle-aged Nando University administrator who greeted me at the train station. "I can't believe it's taken us this long to decommission Ohin. That god is nothing but a headache. We'll be well rid of him."

"On behalf of the Ministry of Divinities, I am honored to assist," I said. It was a formal answer, designed to hide my irritation. The university might want this no-account god removed, but it was clear from their timetable that despite the service I'd be rendering them, they wanted me gone as soon as possible too. They'd scheduled the decommissioning directly upon my arrival and had issued me a ticket back to the capital for later that day. Consequently, I'd had to travel in my regalia, and now I found myself sweating, despite the autumn chill, and breathless in my weighty garments from trying to match Mr. Haksola's rapid pace.

Eventually, Mr. Haksola became aware that I was flagging and slowed down. "I'm sorry everything is so rushed," he said. "Would you believe the only time that our grounds maintenance people have free to dismantle Ohin's shrine before... Well, the only time they have free is shortly after you finish? Ridiculous. Too bad we realized so late that the decommissioning step had to come first!" An odd laugh escaped from him. "Thank you for accommodating us."

Once we slowed down, I noticed our progress across the campus was attracting attention. The silver bells along the hem of the black velvet cape of my office were jingling with each step I took. Inevitably people's gazes traveled up to the seal of the Ministry of Divinities, embroidered in silver on the cape's left breast. Some seemed merely curious, but on a number of faces I saw disapproval, maybe even anger.

"How have Ohin's followers taken the news of his decommissioning? Does he have many active worshipers?" I had assumed he wouldn't. The brief I'd read on him, a mere two sentences, had characterized him as a very minor, very local god of irresponsibility and excess.

Mr. Haksola snorted. "Not many, though they cause the university a surprising amount of trouble. In general, they pass their days either intoxicated or hung over. Their opinions are of no consequence."

"But…" I glanced over my shoulder at a middle-aged woman, well dressed in a fur-trimmed coat, who'd grimaced ostentatiously as we passed. She was no delinquent mischief maker, and neither were the other well-heeled passersby whose reactions I'd noted. I put this to Mr. Haksola.

His brow furrowed momentarily then relaxed as comprehension dawned. He chuckled. "It won't be Ohin that they're upset about. Most people consider Ohin a joke—university administrators excepted. No, people must see your robes and assume you're here to decommission Amaya."

I was flabbergasted. "The apple goddess? Why on earth would anyone think that? The Ministry doesn't go around randomly decommissioning deities."

Mr. Haksola shrugged. "The public sees a representative of the central government and assumes you're here for something important." He paused. "Decommissioning Amaya would make people very unhappy. She's well loved here in the Northwest."

"The Ministry knows that! She would never be decommissioned." It was dismaying to think my presence could inspire that fear in people. "Amaya's plaque is scheduled to be added to the roster of divine expressions of Abundance at the central shrine to Abundance in the capital," I pointed out.

At my mention of Abundance, Mr. Haksola shook his head ever so slightly.

"This whole move from named deities to Abstractions that the Ministry's embraced is very… People want to worship Amaya, not Abundance."

"The Ministry understands that," I said. "That's why named deities are grandfathered in areas like the Northwest." *For now, anyway.* There had been a lot of wrangling over that decision. I made a mental note to tell my superiors that it appeared to be a wise move.

"I trust the Ministry always to take the local situation into account, and I know it has the best interests of the entire Polity in mind," Mr. Haksola said, in strenuously neutral tones.

A thought occurred to me. Decommissioning Ohin shouldn't take more than an hour, but my train back to the capital wouldn't be arriving until the late afternoon. That left me with time on my hands that I could put to good use.

"Amaya's seminary is at Nando, so there must be a shrine to her on campus, yes?" I asked.

"Oh yes—two, in fact. The one by the library is ancient—it dates back to the earliest days of the university. It's on the historical register!" Mr. Haksola's voice was warm with pride. Nando University is one of the oldest universities in the world. It not only predates the Northwest's joining the Polity, it predates the Polity itself—by more than a thousand years.

"Well then, how about I stop by and pay my respects, once I've finished decommissioning Ohin? Not with all this on, of course. Just in street clothes. Would that set people's minds at ease regarding the Ministry's intentions?"

"That would be a lovely idea," Mr. Haksola said, sounding genuinely enthusiastic. "We could meet at the university guest house and go together."

"I'll see you at the guest house, then," I said.

Mr. Haksola beamed. "I'll send you its coordinates," he said, tapping his unicom. Mine chimed in receipt. "Here, see?" A map flashed onto his clipboard papers. "It's a quick walk from Ohin's shrine, which is...oh. Here, actually. We've arrived."

An iron railing cordoned off the supposed sacred space of Ohin's shrine—no more than a patch of bare earth with one stunted pine tree hunched miserably at the back—which was jammed between the long, low grounds maintenance sheds and the overflowing refuse bins of one of the student refectories. All manner of undergarments dangled from the lower branches of the pine tree, and the ground was littered with crushed cans and broken bottles, except by the pine, where a girl in the drab coveralls that students across the Polity like to wear in solidarity with the working class was picking up some of the rubbish. She looked up at our approach, eyes widening as she caught sight of me. She scowled and hurried off.

"That's surprising. Usually Ohin's devotees are breaking bottles here, not tidying them up." Mr. Haksola's lips compressed in disapproval. "This shrine is a blot on the university's good name. In truth, I'm embarrassed to have you see it. If decommissioning were possible from a distance—"

"It's all right; it's fine," I assured him.

My feet tingled as we made a quick circuit of the shrine precinct.

"Interesting," I said. "Despite the desecration, Ohin is still very present."

Mr. Haksola wrinkled his nose. "The less promising students keep him alive. What you take for desecration are their signs of devotion. These"—he nudged a spent prophylactic with the tip of his right shoe—"are his devotees' thank you notes."

I stifled a laugh. It was clearly very distressing for Mr. Haksola.

"Well," I said, bringing my hands together, "I should get started."

Mr. Haksola surveyed the shrine again. "You're all right by yourself?"

I smiled. "I prefer it that way, actually. There's not much to see," I added hastily, thinking I saw disappointment on Mr. Haksola's face.

He replied, "No, that's fine, quite fine. Just so long as it gets done. You're sure you can do it in just one session?"

"One session is all it takes for waning or forgotten gods." I assessed the tingling in my feet. "Ohin seems more vigorous than the Ministry's brief indicated, but as a minor deity with just one point of worship, he still shouldn't be a problem."

Mr. Haksola ran a hand through his stiff, graying hair and shifted his weight.

"I'll get the job done," I promised.

"All right; good. Thank you." He hesitated a moment more, then gave a nod and headed off, shoulders hunched like an anxious heron.

Different decommissioners have different ways of going into trance state. I like to walk the perimeter of the shrine of the deity I'm decommissioning, reciting the names of the gods that were worshipped in my grandparents' day in the Sweet Harbor district of the capital. I usually follow that with a recitation of the principle Abstractions. This time, the beads of divine resin I'd taken from my satchel grew warm in my fists before I'd finished with the Sweet Harbor gods. I waited until smoke was seeping from between my fingers, then scattered the beads at the shrine's four corners. An intense fragrance filled the air. I stood by the pine tree and waited.

"Oooh, incense. Fancy," said a lounging voice. Ohin manifested as a young, male student, in coveralls like the girl I'd just seen. In the conservative Northwest, young men often wear their hair shorn very short, but Ohin's was long, tied loosely with a ribbon from which strands escaped fetchingly, like the hero of one of the popular melodramas.

"You looking to get laid?" he drawled.

"No," I replied, embarrassed at the mix of inappropriate thoughts and feelings I was experiencing.

"You sure? You look like you could use it, and I promise you, age is no barrier."

I bristled. Thirty-five is not that old, and I'm generally told I look young for my age. "Yes," I said, "I'm absolutely positive." Blood rushed to my cheeks, and Ohin laughed. *He's a god of delinquency; provocation is in his character description,* I reminded myself. I took a deep breath.

"I'm here on business."

The god leaned back on the stunted pine and raised his eyebrows in silent inquiry.

"The university administration has decided it's time for you to retire. I'm here to decommission you."

Ohin's expression went from insolent to flinty.

"The university administration can shove hot pokers up their asses," he said, his words accompanied by a wave of searing heat. It was unnerving; I had not expected resistance, much less harm, in this encounter, but it seemed likely that my body had taken some damage. Nothing life threatening—I'd deal with it later. There was no way I was going to let this punk god know he'd surprised me. He was still scowling and staring me full in the face, reminding me of nothing so much as a defiant child, waiting to see what punishment he'd earned.

"Look," I said, summoning what patience I could muster. "The students are going to keep on skipping class and partying whether you're here to preside over it or not. Think of decommissioning as a well-earned vacation. Other decommissioned gods tell me that living as mortals is quite relaxing."

"Well that's dandy for them, but I've already had my mortal existence," Ohin said sulkily.

There was only one way Ohin could have already had a mortal existence: he would have to have been a mortal who was raised to godhood.

"You're telling me you're an apotheosis?"

Ohin executed a graceful bow, though his expression was still petulant.

"Whatever for?" I asked—never mind that the question was inherently disrespectful. "And when?" It seemed inconceivable.

"Dunno. I don't remember." Same sulky tone, but with something like sadness underneath. "*They* don't remember," he said, flicking at one of the pine tree's dangling undergarments, "so how am I supposed to?"

Ohin's worshipers weren't the only ones who didn't remember when or why he had ascended to godhood. The Ministry's brief had made no mention of the fact either. It had, in fact, failed to prepare me for anything I'd experienced at the shrine. It was a singularly worthless document.

"You don't remember anything at all about your past?" I pressed.

Ohin waved a careless hand. "Guaranteed, there must have been plenty of this," he said, tipping his head back, miming drinking. "And plenty of this—" Before I could stop him, he'd pulled me close, pressing his lips and hips against mine. Everything firm within me seemed to liquefy. Just as quick, he released me. I gasped and staggered back.

"Had to have been lots of that, right? That's who I am."

Was he asking me for confirmation? I could barely hear his words over the plucked-string vibrations of desire still thrumming through me. When I finally collected myself, Ohin was staring at me with a mixture of amusement and disbelief.

"You most definitely need to get laid," he said.

"It's you who's the issue here, not me," I replied, with as much hauteur as I could manage. I shifted my cape so it sat more neatly on my shoulders, but the jingling of its bells as I moved mocked me, given what I had to say next: "I have to leave you for now."

"So, I get to remain king of the class cutters? Not enough punch in your Polity toolbag to take me down?"

He was back to insolent, and I could feel a headache coming on as the trance began to lift. "The Ministry of Divinities doesn't know the first thing about you," I admitted. "I'll be back when I have more information."

"If you want to get to know me," he began, a suggestive grin illuminating his face. It faded, and in its wake, Ohin looked tired. It crossed my mind that apotheoses might not be as immune to the weight of time as other divinities. "But suit yourself." He stooped, picked up an unbroken bottle, tossed it in the air, and caught it. "I'll be here." He melted away with the last of the trance.

The first thing I became aware of as I returned to myself was that the blast of Ohin's displeasure had left me with sunburn on my face, and this despite my sun-tolerant southern complexion. The second thing was a tough-faced, middle-aged woman with a badge on her tan coveralls and a crew of five younger men and women standing beside an open utility vehicle and armed with mattocks, shovels, and a chain saw.

"You done now, ma'am?" the crew chief asked, her broad Northwestern accent very different from Mr. Haksola's cultured tones.

"No, actually. I'm afraid not." My cheeks burned as much from the shame of the admission as from Ohin's anger.

"Thing is, if we don't do this now, we're not going to be able to do it at all," the chief said. "Look." She pulled a square of paper from her pocket and unfolded it.

"See? Next period we're scheduled to join crews five, six, and seventeen to help erect the stands for the groundbreaking ceremony." *Infinitesimal Materials Center — Construction Groundbreaking,* the schedule read.

"You may as well go straight there," I said, pressing my cool fingers to my hot face. "The god Ohin is still resident here, and he won't take kindly to your dismantling his shrine."

"That joker? I don't believe he's even for real," scoffed one of the crew members. "Boss, we should just do the job anyw—"

A blinding flash of light cut the man off abruptly as he stepped over the metal rail. When my vision cleared, the man was lying on the ground, his face and chest blistered. All that remained of the top portion of his coveralls were blackened bracelets of cloth at his wrists.

"Mother of Apples!" breathed one of the man's crewmates, and two others dropped their tools and rushed to pull him from the shrine precinct. The man's eyes fluttered and he groaned. I exhaled pent-up breath. He was alive.

"Who'd believe the bastard had it in him," muttered another crewmate.

"Why didn't you get rid of him?" the chief demanded. "Isn't that what you're here for?"

"I wasn't given sufficient information," I said, helpless anger welling up in me.

"Oh yeah? Well now I'm short a crew member," she said, gesturing at the stricken man as if I hadn't just witnessed what had happened. Then, in softer tones, she said, "Laktari, you with us? You here?"

"You should get his burns treated," I advised. "They're serious."

The crew chief shot me a disgusted look, but ordered the others to lift Mr. Laktari into the vehicle. I took a deep breath and headed for the guest house. My mood wasn't helped by my one glance back at the shrine. The student who'd been there when I arrived was back, and staring at me intently.

On the way to the guest house, I sent several requests to the Ministry database. The procedure for decommissioning an apotheosis involves assuring them that the special circumstances surrounding their deification have either changed or—when a special mandate (protection, championship) is involved—been fulfilled, but that assumes those circumstances are known. Had any other decommissioners dealt with an apotheosis of unknown origin? And were those two sentences in Ohin's brief really all the Ministry knew about him? I was hoping some queries about Nando's history would turn up something more.

Mr. Haksola was waiting for me at the guest house, pacing by the door, his rounded shoulders

FRANCESCA FORREST

nearly up to his ears. He straightened when he caught sight of me and held out his wrist, pointing at his unicom accusingly.

"I've had three messages. Three! From the unit sixteen work crew, from the infirmary, and from my superiors. That's three ways that I've been told that Ohin is still with us. Still with us, and— and— injuring people." He blinked rapidly and swallowed. His anger and frustration I understood, but why did he seem frightened?

"Nobody told me Ohin was an apotheosis," I said angrily. "Did you know he was? Does anyone at this university know anything about this god who's been resident on campus for—well, for how many years? Can anybody answer me that? There's virtually nothing on him in the Ministry of Divinities' database, and no mention of him in Nando University's file at the Ministry of Education, either—I checked on my way back here. And it's vital information. An apotheosis is a special case; they can't be decommissioned in the ordinary way."

"Th-they can't? I... We... I didn't know that," Mr. Haksola said. Northwesterners are disconcertingly pallid at the best of times, but at that moment, Mr. Haksola had gone an alarming shade of gray. Abruptly, he pushed open the door to the guest house and held it for me. He nodded to the attendant at the reception desk and slid into a seat at one of the tables in the common room. I joined him.

"*Did* you know that Ohin was an apotheosis?" I asked.

The question appeared to add to Mr. Haksola's distress, because his hands trembled like an old man's as he attempted to pour hot tea from the pot the attendant brought us.

"Yes. Yes, I suppose I did," he said. He pushed one cup toward me and drank down his own before mine had cooled enough for me to even begin.

I poured him a refill and took a sip of my own. "Do you know the circumstances of his elevation?" I asked.

Mr. Haksola had just raised his cup to his lips. At my question, his hand shook so violently the tea spilled. He set down the cup and looked around for the attendant. "You need this information to decommission him?" he asked.

"Yes, I do."

Mr. Haksola took a breath, took a sip of tea— successfully this time.

"Maybe you know that in ancient times, all instruction at Nando University was oral," he began, looking to me for confirmation.

"Yes, I did know that."

He nodded and continued, "By the time the Northwest joined the Polity, only the seminary of Amaya persisted in oral instruction. Finally, two hundred years ago, the Ministry of Education mandated complete compliance with its standards for all institutions of higher learning—no exceptions. Amaya's novices were required to pass a Ministry-approved written examination. When the seminary failed to submit an exam for approval, the Ministry said it would send one."

I winced inwardly. The Polity has a way of rolling right over passive resistance.

"This apparently displeased some of the novices—maybe they were good at parroting prayers but couldn't get the knack of writing, or maybe their learning was impeded by pursuits not worthy of their time. Be that as it may, rather than face the humiliation of failing the exam, those novices tried to stop it from being administered.

"Back then, there was no railroad in these parts; examiners from the Ministry of Education traveled all the way from the capital by palanquin, carrying the exams in a lacquer box bound with iron. Disguised as bandits, the novices attacked the delegation and tried to make off with the box, but the delegation's security detail easily repelled them and pursued them when they fled. One bandit turned and fought, which gave his comrades a chance to escape, but that one lost his life."

"Ohin," I said, my lips tingling where his had touched them.

Mr. Haksola inclined his head ever so slightly in acknowledgment. "His classmates must have elevated him out of sympathy for his foolhardy attempt and his unfortunate end," he said dryly.

I frowned. "That's not possible. It takes great spiritual authority to deify someone. There's no way students could pull that off, not even seminarians."

"They couldn't?" Mr. Haksola's lips twitched as he tried to frame a reply. "Then I, I guess…"

"What do you mean, 'you guess'? Doesn't the university have a record of the event?"

A half-choked laugh escaped from Mr. Haksola. "It's ironic," he said, "given what I just said about the written exam, but—" A chiming sound interrupted him. He glanced at his unicom. "That's my alert. Afternoon rites are about to start at

Amaya's shrine. Can you change quickly?" He turned to the attendant. "Caretaker! Can the decommissioner use the suite you mentioned? And she'll need it for the night too—the university will pay."

Further discussion of the Ohin situation had to wait. I hurriedly changed and accompanied Mr. Haksola to the historic shrine to the Northwest's goddess of apples.

Prayers were just beginning when we arrived. Given that it was the last day before exams, I wasn't expecting many students to be present, but there was a healthy crowd of them, as well as a good number of people from Nando City—parents with small children, a few young unmarrieds, and elders as well.

All were kneeling on patterned rush mats arranged in concentric half-circles around an ancient apple tree. A statue of Amaya, carved in apple wood and sheathed in gold leaf, sat in the first fork of the venerable tree, facing the mats. An apple rested in her left hand; her right she extended to her worshipers.

Mr. Haksola brought me to the closest half-circle of mats, which appeared to be reserved for dignitaries, and we knelt between a distinguished-looking man with a trim white beard and one of the shrine attendants.

Mr. Haksola joined in the call and response between the priest and the faithful, eyes closed. I closed my own eyes, intending to sit in respectful silence, but a gently admonishing voice said, "Why are you tormenting poor Ohin, hmm? Such a faithful and good friend to me."

My eyes flew open. There before me stood the statue of Amaya, her gold-leaf-covered hands on her gold-leaf hips, her head canted to the left as she gazed into my face. The statue was tiny: On my knees, I looked her directly in the eye.

I could tell by the silence and stillness around us that I was in trance state again.

"It's merely my job, honored one," I said. "I came at the request of the university." Her steady stare demanded more from me. "Apparently he makes trouble for them." Under the gaze of the goddess, this seemed like a weak reason. Why was the university rushing to decommission Ohin now, when they had been content to put up with his presence for two hundred years?

"You must celebrate him before sending him into oblivion," the goddess said—a binding injunction.

"Yes, honored one. *Let my actions be guided by your desire.*" The words tumbled from my lips, not against my will, but not exactly with its consent, either. My will, in this situation, was irrelevant. A disquieting realization.

The goddess smiled, and the gold that clad her became an apple-blossom-scented radiance that enveloped me, then spread outward, thinning and fading.

And then it was gone. I was no longer in trance. The priest and the shrine attendants were standing where Amaya had been, and the other worshipers clustered around us a respectful few steps away, leaning in eagerly.

"Madam. Am I right in understanding that you are the guest from the Ministry of Divinities?" the priest inquired.

I nodded, still too disoriented to venture words.

"And...were you communing, just now, with Amaya?"

"Yes, your grace," I managed.

The crowd's murmuring picked up; in my confused state, it sounded like the rustling of leaves in the wind.

"May I inquire… Would you be so kind…" the priest left the words hanging, and I realized I was being invited to share Amaya's words.

"The message concerned the decommissioning of Ohin," I began, which elicited a strangled moan from Mr. Haksola.

"Did she say Ohin?" I heard a woman ask. "Isn't that the dropout god?"

The priest waved a hand, whether to silence the crowd or in dismissal of anything pertaining to Ohin, I wasn't sure. He was focused on something else. In urgent tones he asked, "Your last words. What were the last words you said?"

"What?"

"You said, 'It's merely my job, honored one' and 'Apparently he makes trouble for them' and 'Yes, honored one,' and then what?"

"I said, '*Let my actions be guided by your desires.*'" The words felt strange in my mouth. The priest was staring at me with a terrible intensity.

"What language is that? What does it mean?" he asked, a tremble in his voice.

My mouth went dry: We were speaking the Polity's national language. There are regional dialects, of course, and in isolated areas or recently incorporated territories, people may speak other tongues. But I grew up in the capital and have only ever spoken the national language and market slang.

"I didn't realize I was speaking an unknown tongue. The words were just…the right words to answer the goddess with."

"Can you translate them?"

I could feel the words forming in my mind. *Now stop,* I told myself. *And say them in the national language.* I did.

The priest drew a notepad and stylus from his robes and inscribed rapidly.

"Now please say again the words that the goddess spoke," he requested. I complied, and he repeated the words back to me. Only then could I hear the difference between the words Amaya had spoken and their translation.

The priest turned to the shrine attendants. "Now you say it," he ordered. His stylus wavered over his notepad for a moment as the attendants repeated back the phrase. Then, with determination, he inscribed the words. The attendants looked uneasy.

"Your grace, should you?" one asked.

"Yes," the priest replied, in no uncertain tones. "This is a gift from Amaya; we must not let it be lost again." He turned to me. "I believe those words are from the ancient ceremonial tongue, the language of worship of Amaya. It was never written down—"

"It was sacrilege to write it down," murmured the attendant who had spoken up moments before, but the priest ignored her.

"—and it was lost in the years after the seminary abandoned oral instruction," he continued. "It was easier to teach in the Polity vernacular, especially since the examinations were in the vernacular. We've had no way to reconstruct Amaya's tongue—until now. Are you staying here long? Amaya blessed you once; perhaps she will share more words with you."

Thoughts and questions were flying through my head. Of course, the Ministry of Education would have insisted that the exam be in the national language. Amaya had called Ohin her faithful and good friend. Had *she* opposed the move from oral instruction? As a goddess, had she seen what would be lost? Was she the one who had elevated Ohin?

I knew where I needed to go for answers. "I think I may have an even better way to learn more words," I said to the priest, getting to my feet.

Most worshipers, realizing no more divine communications were imminent, had left the shrine. The distinguished-looking man to Mr. Haksola's left, who'd been following our conversation with an expectant brightness, chose that moment to speak. "Your grace, it's about the exam-blessing ceremony. I sent you a tentative schedule—did you have a chance to look at it?"

The priest looked torn.

"I'll tell you what I learn," I said quickly. "I hope to have more to share this evening." We linked unicoms so I'd be able to be in touch, and then Mr. Haksola and I excused ourselves. I headed for the guest house to collect my regalia, Mr. Haksola hurrying alongside me.

"You're going back to Ohin's shrine, I suppose?" he inquired. Sweat was beading on his forehead and temples; he looked unwell.

"Of course I am! I still have a job to finish, and—"

Mr. Haksola interrupted me. "The university would like to cancel the decommissioning—you don't need to bother. The fee will still be remitted to the Ministry of Divinities of course, but please don't trouble yourself any further. Relax at the guest house. Or maybe you'd like a tour of the campus? I can arrange to have someone take you around."

I stopped in my tracks and crossed my arms. Mr. Haksola blinked twice, but set his jaw.

"What do you mean, the university wants to cancel the decommissioning?" I demanded. "An hour ago you were furious that I hadn't accomplished it, and now you want to abandon it? Are you authorized to make that decision? Because I can't believe your superiors have had such a complete change of heart during the time we were at Amaya's shrine."

Mr. Haksola closed his eyes. "Yes. I have the authority. I'll take responsibility for this." It was as if he were confessing to a capital offense.

"But why?" I asked. I thought of what had just happened at Amaya's shrine — the goddess's words of praise for Ohin. "It's because of Amaya, isn't it. She elevated him, and you don't want to cross her." But as soon as I said it, doubt flooded my mind. Why would Amaya deify her faithful and good friend as a champion of failures and dropouts?

"No!" Mr. Haksola's whole body quivered with the strength of his denial. "How can you even suggest such a thing? It has nothing to do with

Amaya. She couldn't possibly have created such a worthless god."

"Well someone did. And Ohin was a novice in her seminary."

"A lackluster novice who tried to sabotage an exam he couldn't pass!" Mr. Haksola said, shaking his head.

We resumed walking toward the guest house.

"This is the situation," Mr. Haksola said in a rush. "Tomorrow a joint delegation from three government ministries is coming for the groundbreaking of the new Infinitesimal Materials Center. It's a real coup to have a premier research facility located here at Nando. We didn't want anything going wrong, and certainly nothing that would—" His mouth twisted miserably. "I know there are some in the Ministry of Education who think Nando puts too much stock in its ancient glory, but this university fully supports the Polity, and we don't want anything—or anyone—to detract from receiving its full support in return. We were hoping decommissioning Ohin would be a simple matter, but clearly it isn't. So please just leave it."

"You wanted Ohin decommissioned because you thought he'd make a bad impression on the visiting delegation?" I asked, incredulous. "You do know that there's a state-sanctioned Abstraction of Mischief, don't you? And there are students who overindulge and flunk out on every campus in the Polity. The delegation won't give Ohin or his followers a second thought."

"Maybe not at any other time of year," Mr. Haksola said in a low voice, "but Ohin always gets up to mischief at exam time."

"Ohin? The god himself? Not his followers?"

Mr. Haksola made a sour face. "The mischief is miraculous in nature; it couldn't be his followers." He drew a tremulous breath. "The pranks always involve some kind of desecration of the national flag."

I pondered this. It's true that the Polity doesn't take kindly to seditious acts, especially ones that could be interpreted as attacks on national unity. I could understand the university's wanting to eliminate a source of potential trouble.

"I wish you'd told me from the start that Ohin was an apotheosis," I said with a sigh. "If I'd known, I could have come better prepared."

Mr. Haksola's face was a mask of defeated resignation. "It seemed better not to mention

Ohin's initial…delinquent act. I didn't know that you would need the information."

My heart contracted. I was a Polity official. Of course Mr. Haksola hadn't wanted to share Ohin's story with me.

We had arrived back at the guest house.

"All right," I said. "I understand. I won't decommission him, but I am going back to his shrine. He still speaks Amaya's ceremonial language. If I can get him to share more of it, maybe the seminary can recreate it."

Mr. Haksola's face had gone that awful gray shade again. "Please don't stir him up. That's all I ask. For the university's sake. For the Northwest's sake."

I reached out and clasped Mr. Haksola's clammy hand. "I won't stir things up," I said.

Mr. Haksola nodded once, his head down between his shoulders, and took his leave.

In the privacy of the suite Mr. Haksola had reserved for me, I made a new search, this time of the Ministry of National Unity's database, for documentation relating to the exam incident two hundred years ago. There was a brief report: The government had categorized it as an act of delinquency rather than sedition. All the same, they'd posted a unit of the national police to campus to keep an eye on things for a full year. Then I accessed Nando University's own historical archive, looking for any reference to Ohin's apotheosis, but there was nothing. I tried searching on reports of vandalism or mischief making around exam time, and sure enough, each year, stretching back over the decades, there was a cryptic notation: "Damages [O]," with no further explanation.

I sighed. So, for most of the year, Ohin indulged students in their excesses, but on the anniversary of his death, he pranked the Polity. Even without knowing exactly what sort of prank he might get up to, it was easy to imagine it metastasizing into an ugly incident if the visiting delegation caught wind of it, or worse, witnessed it. And now that I had promised not to go through with the decommissioning, I was powerless to prevent it from happening.

Then there was Amaya's injunction. Would she still want me to celebrate Ohin now that I wasn't "sending him into oblivion"?

For the second time that day, I donned my decommissioner's regalia and returned to Ohin's shrine. I hadn't made even half a circuit of the grounds before the beads of divine resin began to smoke.

Ohin looked different this time. His fashionable long hair was gone—in fact, all his hair was gone. His head was shaved in the manner of a novice, and in place of the coveralls, he was wearing full, undyed woolen skirts, sashed at the waist, that I recognized from old scrolls as historical garb of priests of Amaya.

"What have you done, decommissioner?" he demanded. "I was peacefully enjoying an eternity of lighthearted debauchery, and suddenly—" He ran his hand over his shaven scalp and turned slowly so his skirts unfurled like a flower around him. "Suddenly this." His jaw clenched. "Why did you have to make me remember?" He closed his eyes, leaned his head back against his shrine's dejected pine.

"It wasn't me," I said. "It was Amaya."

Ohin pushed away from the tree, eyes wide now. "*Lady of sunshine and sweet rain,*" he whispered reverently.

The words tingled in my ears.

"What did you say? What is that?" I asked.

"*Lady of sunshine and sweet rain,*" he repeated. "It's from one of the salutations—how did I forget that? It's one of our names for her." The tenderness and respect in his voice was totally unlike what I'd heard from him during the morning.

"*Lady of sunshine and sweet rain,*" I said, treasuring the feel of the words on my tongue. I pressed record on my unicom and said the words again, then hit replay. A flattened, reedy version of my voice filled the precinct. Ohin lifted an eyebrow.

"You're teaching your bracelet sacred words?" he asked. "I've heard people say adornment can be a form of prayer, but I've never heard of asking the adornment to do the praying."

"This will let me share the words with Amaya's head priest, here at the university," I explained. "If I forget, it will remember."

Ohin frowned. "Why in Amaya's own name would her head priest want to hear these words from you?"

"Because they've been lost for almost two hundred years," I said, pained by an obscure sense of culpability.

"What do you mean, 'lost'?" As Ohin spoke, the bottles and cans by his feet rattled ominously, and I smelled ozone.

"Do you remember stealing the first written exams?" I asked.

Ohin's gaze was distant. "Writing is a clever tool, but Amaya's words must never be chained by it. It's sacrilege," he said, barely audible.

"But the exam wasn't in Amaya's language. It was in the vernacular."

Ohin looked at me in confusion. From the waking world beyond our communion I dimly heard laughing voices call out, "Ohin, brother, you've gotta grant us a blessed high, because the statics exam is gonna sink us!" There was a tinkling sound as glass shattered somewhere in the shrine, and someone said, "Seven hells, that's a Polity decommissioner—let's get out of here!"

Ohin's form rippled, and for a moment he was again the dashing gallant I'd met in the morning, smiling knowingly and blowing a kiss in the direction of the retreating voices. But then he shimmered again, reappearing as the shaven-headed novice, his brow still knitted in incomprehension.

"You didn't know the exam would be in the vernacular?" I asked.

He shook his head slowly. His lips parted, but he didn't speak.

A bone-penetrating sadness settled on me as I finished the story. "Eventually instruction at the seminary switched to the national language too," I said. "Amaya's sacred language fell into disuse and…was forgotten."

The scent of ozone grew even more intense. There was a rumble like thunder, a flash like lightning, and a blackened bough from the shrine pine appeared in Ohin's fist, still festooned with underwear. His eyes fell on the torn lace of one of the undergarments, and briefly he reverted to the god of dropouts. "A boy just wants to spend his time with liquor on his lips and a lover in his arms," he said, flashing a smile that was replaced almost instantly by an expression of desolation as he became again the youthful novice. He threw down the bough.

"What have I become?" he asked, tears standing in his eyes. He wiped them away with the heels of his hands.

"I won't fail Amaya twice," he said, and disappeared, ripping me out of trance state and leaving me shivering in the cold, long light of late afternoon.

At the other end of the shrine precinct stood the girl from this morning, a heavy book bag slung across her chest and her arms folded tightly against its strap. "Why'd you have to do it?" she demanded as I approached. "Why'd you destroy Ohin?" Her Northwestern accent was thick, but what caught my attention were her eyebrows, which swooped beautifully, expressively—angrily—downward, and her lips, which reminded me of the statue of Amaya.

"As a matter of fact, I haven't done anything," I snapped. "The university has decided not to decommission Ohin after all."

It was strange that she had said *destroy* instead of *decommission*. Did she know that Ohin was an apotheosis? Now wasn't the time to ask. Somewhere, Ohin was seeking retribution for a two-hundred-year-old wrong.

The girl gave a decisive nod of the head. "Good. Decommissioning him was a stupid, small-hearted idea. Ohin never hurt anyone."

"Maybe not in the past, but I'm afraid he's about to, and if he does, it's going to make big trouble," I said.

The girl snorted. "Oh sure. What's he going to do, spark an outbreak of lovers' curse, or alcohol poisoning? People get into that trouble themselves;

all he does is bless their actions. Not everyone is cut out for scholarship."

"*You* seem to be," I said, nodding at her book bag.

The girl's face reddened, and she shifted the bag. "Exams start tomorrow… I'm trying to keep a scholarship."

"Exactly. You're not a typical Ohin devotee. They break bottles here. You come and clean them up. They're begging favors from him, but you're here defending him."

She dropped her head and murmured something I couldn't hear.

"What's that?" I asked.

"I know things about him, that's all," she flared, then looked away again.

"I do too," I said. "I know he was a novice in Amaya's seminary before he was deified."

The girl's eyes widened, then narrowed. "That administrator told you," she said angrily. "He shouldn't have. That knowledge isn't supposed to be shared with anyone who would harm Ohin."

"Deifying Ohin harmed Ohin!" I said.

The girl laughed. "Leave it to a Polity decommissioner to call deification harm. It would have been better for him just to have been forgotten? Deifying him is probably the only generous thing the university has ever done for a failing student."

The university had deified him? I stared at the girl, stunned. But with that piece in place, the picture was much clearer.

"Ohin wasn't a failing student," I said slowly. "That's just the story that got put out to satisfy Polity investigators. The university elevated Ohin as a deity of dropouts and debauchery to overwrite his true past. It was cover for the institution, not a tribute to a dead novice. But now that act has come back to haunt them. If you do care about him—and about the future of the university—you have to help me stop whatever Ohin's about to do. And then, maybe, we can honor him in a way he deserves."

In the distance, an electronic chime sounded the hour. Long shadows from the refectory refuse bins now stretched across the shrine grounds. The girl searched my face.

"You're serious," she said.

"Very," I said.

She bit her lip. "All right," she said at last. "I'll help. My name's An-maya."

"'Of Amaya'?" I guessed.

She nodded. "It's a super-common girl's name around here. My parents have a big devotion to Amaya. Myself, I prefer the Abstractions."

I filed that piece of information away for later; it was an interesting contrast to what Mr. Haksola had said—maybe a generational difference.

"What should I call you?" An-maya asked.

"I'm Decommissioner 37."

An-maya made a face. "You give up names when you join the Ministry?"

"No; it's just policy to… Look, never mind: You can call me Sweeting."

"Sweeting? That's your name?"

"It's a childhood nickname," I said, and before An-maya could laugh or ask more questions, I told her what had happened at her namesake's shrine and how Ohin had reacted when he learned about the loss of Amaya's sacred language.

"So, he stole the exams to prevent a sacrilege, but it ended up being for nothing. He lost everything, even himself," An-maya burst out.

I nodded. "And just now, before he departed, he said he wasn't going to fail Amaya a second time. I'm afraid he's going to attack the delegation that's arriving tomorrow for the Infinitesimal Materials Center groundbreaking. The coincidence of Polity officials arriving more or less on the anniversary of his death and elevation has to be too tempting to pass up."

"Usually he settles for things like causing the Polity flag to appear on all the sheets of toilet paper in the dormitories," An-maya muttered.

"Usually he hasn't just remembered who he is and what's been lost," I pointed out. I rested the toe of my boot on the charred pine bough Ohin had flung down. "The thing I'm wondering is, when and where he'll make his attack."

"That's easy. Tarta Pass," An-maya said, without hesitation.

The name meant nothing to me.

"You came here by train, right? Do you remember, maybe twenty minutes before arriving at Nando City, a spot where the mountains pressed in on both sides? That's Tarta Pass. It's the only break in the mountains for leagues if you're coming from the southeast. Before the railroad was put through, an ancient highway followed that route. It's got to be where Ohin attacked the delegation two hundred years ago."

"How quickly can we get there?" I asked.

"It's the end of the work day. The roads are going to be crowded at this hour, and you don't have a vehicle... It'll be dark before we get anywhere."

I imagined the two of us scrabbling around blindly in a mountain pass. It seemed hopeless.

"Unless..." An-maya hesitated.

"Unless what?"

"Can you ride a moto-velo? There's a rental place near campus and a whole network of trails — we could bypass the roads entirely. One trail comes out on a lookout spot above the pass." An-maya pressed her palms together and brought them to her lips, prayer fashion. "Assuming there are moto-velos available, then if we go at top speed, we should get there while it's still light."

"Let's go then!" I said, gesturing for her to lead the way.

"But can you really ride, dressed like that? Your cape looks, uh, inconvenient."

"I'll manage."

"I didn't think Ohin could do anything off campus," An-maya said as we walked through the university's main gate and out into Nando City.

"He's a god. Even if the terms of his apotheosis limit his sphere of influence, I'm sure he can overcome the restriction if he has a reason to try, and he's got one. I'm curious: How did you come to know as much about him as you do?"

She shrugged. "I'm a history major; I like finding out stuff about the past. At Nando, everywhere you look, there's some weird bit of history to notice, and one thing I noticed was that Ohin's shrine had no plaque. And it was so sad looking! I wondered why, so I dug around, but it turns out there's nothing written about him anywhere. I kept poking, though, and eventually I got a call from a retiring professor who told me the story—well, the university's version, anyway. It's been handed down through the generations, but never written down."

"Oral transmission only," I said. The irony wasn't lost on me.

An-maya nodded, then frowned. "You said that elevating Ohin was a way for the university to protect itself, but it seems like a lot of trouble to go to. Wouldn't it have been better to let the whole incident just fade into the past?"

"What Ohin did—it was on behalf of Amaya and the seminary's intellectual freedom," I replied, conscious that even explaining this might be considered borderline seditious. "He lost his life for their sake. If the university hadn't done something to honor him, his vengeful ghost would likely have made trouble. So, they needed to celebrate him, honor him somehow. What better way than by deifying him in a manner that conformed with the version of events that they wanted accepted?"

An-maya's frown deepened. "So wrong," she muttered.

By then we'd arrived at the moto-velo rental, and we were in luck: I was able to rent two, though the proprietor charged overnight fees as it was so late in the day. I paid still more for some battered helmets, which the proprietor claimed were a legal requirement for all riders. An-maya's eyeroll made me doubt this, but we didn't have time for an argument. We donned the helmets, and An-maya mounted one of the moto-velos and revved the engine, enveloping us both in fumy smoke. She took off toward the hills, and I followed close behind her.

After about a half hour of climbing at full throttle, we broke from the dark mountain cypresses into an open area that overlooked Tarta Pass. Yellowed grasses, pink-tinged in the light of the setting sun, rippled in the breeze, and on the far side of the pass the few aspens that hadn't shed their leaves glowed like candles amid the cypresses.

There were already visitors at the lookout. Two young men, students, judging from their coveralls, were reclining in the grass, amid bottles of hard cider and persimmon wine. When we'd dismounted from our moto-velos and the exhaust had cleared, an unmistakable pungent odor told us they were indulging in dreamers-herb as well.

"Coming up by moto-velo is cheating, ladies," one of them drawled. "You're only flash if you hike. Want a puff?" He held out a long, slim clay pipe. "It's Ten Thousand Sunny Days varietal."

"I'm low-tolerance," An-maya said, waving it away. "But if you're offering, I'll have some of that." She pointed at the persimmon wine.

"You've got taste," the other student said, passing An-maya the whole bottle.

She wiped its mouth on the sleeve of her coverall and took a swig. We had just gotten far enough in introductions to learn that the two were named Dila and Derok, and that they were likely to be flunking out of the School of Engineering next term, when Derok pushed himself upright and squinted at me, frowning.

"That one's the divine decommissioner we saw at the shrine," he said. The way he leaned over and cupped his hand by Dila's ear suggested he intended to whisper, but it came out at ordinary volume. Then, to me, in tones of inebriated wonderment rather than accusation, "You're here to decommission Ohin."

"Don't know why you're even bothering," Dila remarked, lying down completely. "We'll just make our petitions to Mischief instead."

"You will, won't you," I said. In a rush of gratitude, I realized Dila's words held the key to a way out of the Ohin mess. But first things first. I came to the edge of the outlook and peered down. Far below were the railroad tracks, silvery parallel lines cutting their way through the mountains.

"I don't know if this is maybe normal for decommissioners, but uh…your bag there is smoking," said Derok, eyeing my satchel, which I'd left on the seat of the moto-velo. I raced over and dumped out the contents. Smoke was rising from my entire remaining supply of divine resin beads.

"Pantheon of deities and Abstractions," I swore under my breath. It had to mean Ohin was present, or near. I tried to recite the litany of Sweet Harbor gods, but all that came to my mind and lips was my assent to Amaya: *Let my actions be guided by your desire.* Not knowing what else to do, I pushed the resin beads to the edges of the lookout. Had I marked out a big enough space? Would the students all go into trance too? There was no way of knowing.

"Isn't that a fire hazard?" asked Derok. The beads were now glowing cherry red. Before I could do anything about them, movement on the tracks below caught my eye: a hunched figure, picking his way delicately along the track, head down as if he were searching for something he'd dropped. Mr. Haksola. At some distance behind him, a work crew followed, periodically clustering to examine the tracks. Had Mr. Haksola, like An-maya, concluded that Ohin was most likely to cause trouble in Tarta Pass? Were he and the work crew on the same mission as we were?

"Ma'am, this stuff is intense," murmured Dila.

The aromatic smoke from the resin beads had completely overpowered the dreamers-herb. I inhaled deeply, and as it filled my lungs, a vision filled my mind: novices in bandit garb, panting, bedraggled, and scrambling toward me up the side of the pass along a narrow path made by deer or wild goats, while from below came the sound of shouts and firearms.

"There's a path down to the tracks—I'm going down. It's probably dangerous; you all stay here," I said.

I lowered myself over the edge of the outlook, then clung to it for dear life as I searched for purchase with my feet. I closed my eyes, willing the vision back into my mind. My feet found firm ground. I opened my eyes and slipped, slid, grabbed, twisted, stumbled, and tumbled to the base of the outlook. Before I could get my bearings, a bruising shower of pebbles and loose stones pelted my head and shoulders, and I realized with alarm that the others had followed me down.

Standing before us, and looking oddly unalarmed, was Mr. Haksola.

"You're here because of Ohin, aren't you—have you found anything?" I asked, still breathless.

"Two hundred years ago, they came by palanquin. Tomorrow they'll travel by train," Mr. Haksola said, a peculiar nonresponse.

"Mr. Haksola? Are you all right?" I waved a hand in front of his face, but he didn't respond.

An-maya said something I couldn't hear, and Dila giggled. Mr. Haksola's gaze turned slowly toward them, and his eyebrows drew together slightly in an expression of mild perplexity. "Mr. Haksola, it's late," I said, a little louder. "What are you doing here?" His head swiveled back my way, and he blinked.

"Foiling sabotage," he said, his voice flat, almost absentminded. Then he perked up a little. "See this?" He opened his left hand to reveal a narrow metal cylinder, such as schoolchildren carry writing styluses in. "It's a remote-control detonator. You could be up in the hills, or even at Nando City Station, and press it, and it would still work."

I licked my lips, swallowed. "Did you...did you find any charges set?"

He looked at me blankly, then turned his attention to the detonator, turning it round in his hand. He ran a finger lightly over one end of it.

"That's what you'd press," he murmured.

"Yes... You need to find the charges and dispose of them—isn't that what you were doing?" I glanced over at the work crew for confirmation of this, and the hairs on the back of my neck stood on end. It was the same crew that had been sent to dismantle Ohin's shrine. Now they stood motionless, their faces vacant.

"No charges," the crew chief said, distant cheer in her voice. "See?" She set down a sturdy metal case, pressed a latch, and opened it. "Empty."

My heart hammered as I recalled the view from the lookout. Had the crew been inspecting the track, or had they been laying charges? Was the case empty because they hadn't discovered any explosives, or because they'd placed explosives that they themselves had brought?

"Any time you want the tracks to go, you'd just press it," Mr. Haksola continued, caressing the tip of the detonator.

"So, maybe best not to fiddle with it," I said, laying a hand on Mr. Haksola's arm. He frowned and jerked his arm away with surprising force.

"Put it down is what the decommissioner's trying to say," said Derok, tackling Mr. Haksola and pinning his arms spread-eagled. I pried the detonator from Mr. Haksola's fingers.

"I don't get it," said Dila plaintively. "What's going on?"

"I think your friend just stopped us from getting blown up," An-maya replied.

"Can you deactivate it or, or disarm it, or do whatever needs to be done to it to keep it from detonating anything?" I asked Derok.

"Yeah, but that still leaves explosives on the tracks," he said, releasing Mr. Haksola and taking the detonator from me.

Being tackled seemed to have brought Mr. Haksola back to himself. He clutched his head and moaned, then, catching sight of me and the others, spluttered out, "Decommissioner, what are you doing here? Who are these young people?"

"We're here for the same reason you are — to prevent Ohin from causing an incident. That is why you're out here, right?"

"I thought — I wanted..." He flinched for no discernable reason, and glanced about furtively.

I turned to the crew chief and put my hands on her shoulders. "I need you to put the explosives you laid down back in that case," I said, staring at her steadily.

She blinked, and her eyes came into focus on my face. She scowled.

"You again. First you mess up my schedule at the shrine and now..." She looked round at the tracks and the dark hills. "What the... What in seven hells are we doing out here?"

"My work—which you're interrupting, *Sweeting.*"

That was Ohin, letting the nickname I'd shared with An-maya fall carelessly from his lips the way only a delinquent god could, but he wasn't presenting as Ohin, divine failure. This was Ohin the angry novice, with his shaved head and full skirts, but now surrounded by a golden light that blotted everything from sight but him and pulled the breath from my lungs. I couldn't hope to deal with him in his glory; I had to bleed off some of his power.

"You're far from your precinct—it must be taxing you," I said, hoping to goad him. "Do you feel attenuated?"

"My weakness is stronger than anything in your bag of tricks," he replied. "Where is that bag, by the way? Ah. On fire, I see." Beyond the aureole of Ohin's radiance, I was dimly aware of a snapping, crackling sound and the dance of flames against the night sky, up on the lookout.

"If you're so powerful, why are you making innocent people do your dirty work for you? Can't manage on your own?"

"Those are not innocent people," he shot back. "*He* employed you to destroy me, and *they* tried to dismantle my shrine."

"That shrine's to a god you should never have become: a layabout, a laughingstock, a minor irritation."

Ohin's aura flared to blinding brightness, accompanied by a blast of heat that sent me staggering back. I heard cries from Mr. Haksola, An-maya, and the others. I touched my face, felt blisters. I blinked but could see nothing.

"You shouldn't taunt me," Ohin said, a disembodied voice in the blackness.

"I'm not taunting; I'm speaking truth. And yet however worthless the god Ohin is, he isn't a murderer, and nor was the novice Ohin. Now, though—this sabotage you're planning will almost certainly kill people." Sight was returning to my eyes; I could make out silhouettes and shades of gray.

"Consider it restitution. They didn't kill just one novice when they killed me; they killed a sacred language—you told me that." Anger still threaded through Ohin's words, but what I felt from him more strongly was grief—and exhaustion. As my vision grew clearer, I saw that his aura had faded entirely. He looked no more substantial than a common graveyard ghost.

In that condition, Ohin was eminently decommissionable, but that had ceased to be my task—when? When Amaya had first manifested? When Mr. Haksola had released me from the obligation? Or maybe from my first encounter with Ohin.

"That language can live again, with your help," I said. "You know all the litanies and prayers. If you were the god of the sacred tongue of Amaya, you could help bring it back to life."

"I'm what the university made me," Ohin said, the embers of his anger brightening, but only for a moment. With alarm, I realized Ohin was very nearly gone.

"They were trying to protect—"

"—their own skins," he interrupted, in bitter tones.

"Yes," I conceded, "but also the students, the institution, Amaya even, from the wrath of the Polity. And in the end, thanks to that self-serving action, you survive to be reborn as a new divinity." My heart was racing as I put the suggestion forward.

Silence. Was he still there?

"I can decommission Ohin, the god of dropouts," I continued. "Your worshipers will easily switch their allegiance to Mischief, which suits the Ministry of Divinities' long-term goals. Mr. Haksola can testify that you've fulfilled the mandate placed upon you at your apotheosis—both the ostensible one and the actual one. Once you are freed of that role, and before your spirit flies from here, I can elevate you with the new mandate. How does that sound to you? Acceptable?"

There was no answer, nothing but the sound of the wind in the cypresses and the crackling of the flames on the lookout.

"Has he died? Have you killed him?" Anger and panic in An-maya's voice.

"Acceptable." Ohin's reply was no more than a whisper in the wind.

With shaking hands, I motioned everyone back a few paces.

"I call on those gathered here to attest to the completion of service of the apotheosis Ohin," I intoned. The flames from the wildfire on the lookout surged higher, and the fragrance of the resin beads enveloped us. Mr. Haksola spoke up firmly, and after the barest hesitation, An-maya and the boys joined in.

Ohin's spirit was lifting, and the air and ground grew cold in mourning for the departure of divinity.

Quickly, before he could disappear, I had to re-apotheosize him. I'd learned the ceremony, but hadn't had to recite the words since my qualifying exams, more than ten years ago. Worse, in that cold-and-growing-colder air, I feared I lacked the spiritual authority to do it. I tried to commandeer Mr. Haksola's—he represented the university, and the university had elevated Ohin in the first place—but only a trickle of authority was flowing from him.

"*Let my action be guided by your desire,* honored one!" I called out. It was a desperate prayer.

An-maya's face sprang into visibility in the gloom, illuminated by a sourceless light. Her expression was uncharacteristically mature and affectionate: The goddess Amaya was gracing us in the body of her namesake.

She spoke. "Thank you, Sweeting, for your good work. Ohin my friend! I call on you to join me. You shall be called Lian, and you will teach the youngsters who serve me the words that delight me."

And there he was again, the novice with the shaved head and woolen skirts, but all the sorrow and anger had departed from him. His face was open and there was wonderment in his eyes.

"You, Haksola Krayik, will proclaim this elevation," ordered Amaya, with An-maya's voice.

"Yes, honored one," gasped Mr. Haksola.

"You, Matene Funa, will oversee the building of precincts for Lian near to my own ancient shrine."

"Yes, honored one," said the work crew chief.

"And you, my addled children, will learn my tongue," the goddess continued, addressing Derok and Dila.

"Begging your pardon, honored one, but we're engineers," said Derok, with astonishing temerity.

"Not very good ones—you should try something new." There was a smile in the words.

"Yes, honored one."

And then the figure of Ohin—now Lian—dissolved into a bright glow. Silent explosions of light at several points along the railroad tracks rose to join that luminous cloud, which condensed into a shooting-star pinprick and disappeared skyward. The light went out from An-maya's face.

"Wait, come back!" she called, whether to Amaya or Lian I wasn't sure.

"I'm calling in that wildfire," the crew chief remarked, tapping her unicom. On the lookout, orange flames reached for the stars.

"Seven hells, the moto-velos!" I said. There was no way we could return the way we'd come. "Looks like we'll be walking back."

"Like the Polity delegation two hundred years ago, only instead of bringing a new exam, we're bringing news of a new god," mused An-maya.

"I hope this is satisfactory… I think this will be satisfactory," Mr. Haksola muttered to himself.

I hoped so too. I was going to have to find an acceptable way to report the results of this assignment to my superiors.

"Let's get going," said Derok. "I'm getting hungry."

We set off toward the university, the scent of divinity still clinging to us.

About the Author

Francesca Forrest is the author of *Pen Pal* (2013), a hard-to-classify novel from the margins, as well as short stories that have appeared in *Not One of Us*, *Strange Horizons*, and other online and print venues. She's currently working on a post-apocalypse novel that focuses on the hope rather than the horror.

She blogs at asakiyume.dreamwidth.org, and you can follow her on Twitter at @morinotsuma.

About the Publisher

Annorlunda Books is a small press that publishes books to inform, entertain, and make you think. We publish short books (novella length or shorter) and collections of short writing, fiction and non-fiction.

Find more information about us and our books online: annorlundaenterprises.com/books or on Twitter: @AnnorlundaInc.

To stay up to date on all of our releases, subscribe to our mailing list at:

annorlundaenterprises.com/mailing-list

Selected Other Titles from Annorlunda Books

The Lilies of Dawn, by Vanessa Fogg, a fantasy novelette about love, duty, family, and one young woman's coming of age.

Tattoo, by Michelle Rene, a novella about a young woman who appears in a cynical post-Judgement Day age, and the band of strangers who find themselves called to keep her safe.

Water into Wine, by Joyce Chng, a sci-fi novella about a family trying to build a life amidst an interstellar war that threatens everything.

Caresaway, by DJ Cockburn, a near future "inside your head" thriller about a scientist who discovers a cure for depression, but finds that it comes at a terrible cost.

Both Sides of My Skin, by Elizabeth Trach, a collection of short stories exploring the reality of pregnancy and motherhood.

Unspotted, by Justin Fox, the story of the Cape Mountain Leopard and the author's own journey to try to see one.

The Burning, by J.P. Seewald, a novella set in the coal country of Pennsylvania, about a family struggling to cope as a slow-moving catastrophe threatens everything they have.

Okay, So Look, by Micah Edwards, a humorous, yet accurate and thought-provoking, retelling of the Book of Genesis.

Don't Call It Bollywood, by Margaret E. Redlich, an introduction to the world of Hindi film.

Hemmed In, a collection of classic short stories about women's lives.

Love and Other Happy Endings, a collection of classic short love stories that all end on a high note.

Academaze, by Sydney Phlox, a collection of essays and cartoons about life in academia.

CPSIA information can be obtained
at www.ICGtesting.com
Printed in the USA
BVHW030443151218
535694BV00002B/636/P